Share Market Dictionary

Disclaimer

The book is in the nature of general comment only and neither purports nor intends to give any advice. It is not designed to replace the advice of a Licensed Financial Consultant or a Stockbroker. It has been prepared without regard to any particular person's investment objectives, financial situation and particular needs. Readers should not act on the basis of any matter in this publication without considering (and if appropriate, taking) professional advice with due regard to their own individual circumstances. The decision to trade and the method of trading is for the reader alone to decide. Direct investing in the stock market can result in financial loss. Historical results are no guarantee of future returns.

Share Market Dictionary

A. Sulthan

PRABHAT PRAKASHAN

Published by
PRABHAT PRAKASHAN PVT. LTD.
4/19 Asaf Ali Road,
New Delhi-110 002 (INDIA)
e-mail: prabhatbooks@gmail.com

ISBN 978-93-5322-309-0
SHARE MARKET DICTIONARY
by Shri A. Sulthan

Edition
2026

Price
₹ 300.00 (Rupees Three Hundred only)

Printed at
Narula Printers, Delhi

Author's Note

Share Market Dictionary has been produced to aid beginners in the challenging task of becoming familiar with new vocabulary and terminology that is used in stock exchanges. This could be a valuable reference tool that can be used when attending seminars, watching or listening to financial programmes and reading the financial market material. The book contains over 500 glossary and 123 commonly used abbreviations and acronyms in finance and the stock market.

—A. Sulthan
contact@iamsulthan.in

Contents

B

C

D

E

H

I

O

P

R

S

T

U

V

W

Y

Z

Acronyms & Abbreviations

A

ABANDON

To not to exercise or sell an option. An investor usually chooses abandonment when the option is out-of-the-money on the expiration date.

ABOVE PAR

The current price above face value. This generally occurs when the coupon paid on the bond is higher than the market interest rate for similar securities. If the investor has purchased the bond above par, he/she will suffer a capital loss upon the bond's maturity since it will only be redeemed at face value.

ACCOUNTS PAYABLE

The company's current liability owed to creditors for goods and services obtained during the normal course of business.

ACCOUNTS RECEIVABLE

Current assets owed to the company for services or goods sold on credit.

ACCRETED INTEREST

The difference between par value of a zero coupon security and its original purchase price. Also known as original issue discount.

ACCRUAL BOND

A bond which is sold at a deep discount to its face value, and pays no coupons. Accrual bonds tend to be illiquid, and very sensitive to changes in interest rates.

ACCRUED INTEREST

The amount of interest the buyer owes to the seller on transactions of fixed income securities, such as most bonds and notes.

ACCUMULATION BOND

A bond sold at a price below its face value which can be redeemed at its face value when matured. Also called discount bond.

ACQUISITION

The act of acquiring control of another corporation, by either stock purchase or exchange. This can be achieved either through hostile or friendly means.

ACTIVE MANAGEMENT

The constant supervision of a portfolio's holdings to maximise gains. Active management by fund managers is one of the benefits of a mutual fund.

ADDRESS

The headquarter's address of the company as provided while listing.

ADVANCED OPTION

It is a complex option strategy.

Also read: Spread Order, Straddle, Strangle, Buy/Write, Sell/Write, and Unwind.

ADVISER

The person or a firm primarily responsible for a fund's day-to-day operation.

AFTER-HOURS TRADING

The buying and selling of securities when the major markets are closed. After-hours trading was once a privilege of institutional investors. However, individual investors can now participate. Stocks are traded after-hours on ECNs, which match buyers and sellers with a computer system in order to execute trades.

AFTER MARKET

Markets in which an investor purchases a security from other investors rather than the issuer, subsequent to the original issuance in the primary market. Also called secondary market.

AGENCY SECURITY

The bills, notes, and bonds issued by the agencies of the government.

AGGRESSIVE GROWTH FUNDS

Mutual funds which focus on small company stocks, their high level of risk is justified by potential for accelerated earnings.

ALL-OR-NONE (AON)

The type of order instructing the execution of the entire order quantity at the stated price (or better), or none of it. This prevents partially filled orders. The difference between All-or-None and Fill-or-Kill (FOK) is that the AON order is left open if the entire order quantity cannot be filled, whereas the FOK order will be cancelled.

ALPHA

The measure of a fund's risk-adjusted return. Alpha is derived by comparing the fund's actual returns and the expected returns as determined by its level of risk (beta). A positive alpha indicates the fund has performed better than expected, while a negative alpha indicates the fund has underperformed.

AMERICAN-STYLE OPTION

An option contract that can be exercised at any time between the dates of purchase to expiration. Most exchange-traded options are American-style.

AMORTISATION

The gradual elimination of a liability in regular payments over a specified period of time. Such payments must be sufficient to cover both principal and interest.

ANNUAL PERCENTAGE RATE (APR)

The total cost of a loan per year, including both interest charges and most or all fees.

ANNUAL PERCENTAGE YIELD (APY)

The total income an investment earns per year. The APY generally represents the total earnings of a cash account such as a money market fund or savings account, or be part of the returns from stocks and bonds, which can also experience capital growth.

ANNUAL REPORT

The audited report of a corporation's year-end financial results and operations filed annually. The report contains information on the company's financial condition, legal liabilities and future plans. Shareholders may obtain a free copy of the Annual Report from the corporation.

ANNUAL REPORT (MUTUAL FUND)

A report that gives an overview of a fund's performance and operations. SEC (Securities and Exchange Commission) requires funds to distribute the report to shareholders at least semi-annually.

ANNUALISED RETURNS

The return on an investment over a specified number of years, calculated as what an investor would have received each year if the cumulative returns were distributed evenly over each year within the specified time period.

APPRECIATION FUNDS

Types of funds that invest in stocks whose value is expected to increase significantly.

ARBITRAGE

Profiting from differences in the price of a security that is traded on multiple markets.

ARMS INDEX–TRADING INDEX (TRIN)

A market indicator used in technical analysis, calculated as follows:

$$\text{Arms Index} = \frac{(\text{No. of advancing issues/No. of declining issues})}{(\text{Total up volume/Total down volume})}$$

A value of less than 1 is considered bullish, greater than 1 bearish.

ARREARAGE

The overdue interest or dividends of a bond or preferred share.

ASIAN FUNDS

A fund that targets primarily the stocks of companies located in Asia. These funds appeal to investors who are bullish on the potential of Asian companies, and want to capitalise on that growth.

ASIAN OPTION

An option whose pay-off depends on the average value of an underlying security over a specified period.

ASK (ASKED PRICE)

The lowest round lot price at which a broker will sell a security.

ASK PRICE (MUTUAL FUNDS)

Also known as the offering price, the ask price is the price at which a mutual fund's shares can be bought. The ask price is calculated by adding a fund's current net asset value per share to its sales charges, if any.

ASSIGNMENT

The receipt of an exercise notice by an options writer that requires him to sell (in the case of a call) or purchase (in the case of a put) the underlying security at the specified strike price.

ASSESSMENT BOND

Municipal bond used for specific projects, to be repaid using tax proceeds collected from those who benefit from the project. Also called special-purpose bond.

ASSET ALLOCATION FUNDS

Funds that seek to provide an optimal mix of stocks, bonds and cash at any given time.

AT-THE-MONEY

An option is at-the-money if the strike price of the option is equal to the market price of the underlying security. For example, if a company's stock is trading at $100, then the company's $100 option is at-the-money.

AUCTION (TREASURY)

The issuance of new treasury bills, notes, and bonds at stated intervals by the central bank of the country.

AUCTION MARKET

A market where buyers and sellers enter bids and offers simultaneously, such as the National Stock Exchange, The New York Stock Exchange, etc.

AUTOMATIC INVESTMENT

A shareholder service that allows the periodic transfer of a present amount from the shareholder's bank account to his or her mutual fund account.

AVERAGE/INDEX

Also known as an index, it is the mathematical calculation that indicates the value of a group of securities. Some of the most famous averages include the Nifty, Dow Jones Industrial Average (DJI) and the New York Stock Exchange Composite.

AVERAGE LIFE

An estimate of the time to maturity for a pool of mortgage-backed securities.

AVERAGE MATURITY

The average time to maturity of securities held by a mutual fund. Changes in interest rates have a greater impact on funds with a longer average life.

AVERAGE VOLUME

Average volume is calculated by dividing the total volume for the previous three months by the number of trading days in the period. Compare this number to the daily volume to see if interest in the security has increased or decreased.

AWAY FROM THE MARKET

On a limit order, a buy order which is lower than the current market price, or a sell order which is higher than the current market price. These orders are held to be executed later, unless they are of the fill-or-kill type.

❐

B

BACK-END LOAD

A special percentage charge assessed when mutual fund shares are redeemed.

BALANCE SHEET

An accounting statement reflecting the firm's financial condition in terms of assets, liabilities and net worth (ownership). The sum of the left side (assets) must be equal to that of the right (liabilities + shareholders' equity), balancing both sides of the statement.

BALANCED FUNDS

Mutual funds that invest in both stocks and bonds in an attempt to provide investors with growth and income.

BANKER'S ACCEPTANCE

A short-term credit investment created by a non-financial firm and guaranteed by a bank as to payment. Acceptances are traded at discounts from face value in the secondary market, and are popular among money market funds.

BANKRUPTCY

The financial state of being unable to pay debts. Bankruptcy laws provide for either the reorganisation or liquidation of corporate business and assets to pay some creditors.

BASIS

The total cost an investor pays to acquire a security or asset. It is used to determine capital gains or losses when the asset is sold.

BASIS POINT

One-hundredth of one per cent, or 0.01%. For example, the decrease of an interest rate from 6% to 5.5% means the loss of 50 basis points.

BEAR

A pessimistic investor who believes a stock or the overall market will decline.

BEAR MARKET

A market in which the prices of securities are generally declining.

BEAR RAID

A situation where traders sell short a security, attempting to drive the price lower.

BEARER SECURITIES

Securities for which no register of ownership is kept by

the issuer. Dividends or interest payments are not received automatically but must be claimed by clipping and returning the coupons attached to the certificate.

BED AND BREAKFAST DEAL

This refers to the sale of share and repurchase on another day. It is done to set up profit or loss for the purpose of tax.

BENCHMARK INDEX

Indicators used to compare and evaluating a fund's performance. The most common benchmark for equity-oriented funds in India is the Nifty and Sensex.

BENEFICIAL OWNER

The owner of a security who is entitled to all the benefits associated with ownership. Clients' securities are often registered in the name of the brokerage firm rather than in the name of the client, but the client remains the real or beneficial owner.

BEST 3-MONTH RETURN

The fund's highest three-month return measured in rolling three-month periods over the past five years.

BETA

Beta measures the volatility of a stock's returns relative to the market index. For example, a beta of 1.3 indicates that a stock tends to move 30% more than the Nifty in the same direction. So, if the Nifty rises 10%, the stock will move higher by 13%; but if the S&P (The Standard & Poor's) falls

10%, the stock will fall 13%. In simple words, a higher beta represents a higher risk in investment.

BID

The highest price buyers have declared that they are willing to pay for a security.

BID/ASK SIZE

The number of shares buyers are willing to purchase at the quoted bid price and the number of shares offered for sale at the quoted ask price.

BLOCK

A large number of shares of a security, usually more than 10,000, traded in a single transaction. This is usually done by institutional investors.

BLOW-OFF TOP

A steep and rapid increase in price followed by a steep and rapid drop in price. This is an indicator seen in charts and used in the technical analysis of stock price and market trends.

BLUE-CHIP

A term used to describe the common stocks of corporations with the strongest reputation for generating earnings and paying dividends.

BOND

1. A debt instrument; a security that represents the

debt of a corporation, a government, or any other entity. A bond is usually long-term in nature (5 to 30 years), to be repaid to investors on a specified date.

2. An investment in a government or corporation which is structured like a loan, the difference being payments are made to individual bondholders rather than to a lending institution. Most bonds offer a regular, scheduled income with relatively low risk, making them attractive to retirees and others living off their investments.

BOND FUND

A type of mutual fund that invests in bond and preferred stocks, providing a stable income with low risk.

BOOK ENTRY

An electronic record of ownership of Treasury or other securities.

BOOK VALUE

A value computed by subtracting the total liabilities from the value of assets on the balance sheet, then dividing by the number of common shares.

BOARD OF DIRECTORS

Individuals elected by a corporation's shareholders to oversee the management of the corporation. The members of a Board of Directors are paid in cash and/or stock, and meet several times each year. Some directors serve on the board of more than one company.

BREADTH OF THE MARKET

A measurement of the number of shares that advance or decline on a trading day.

BREAKOUT

A rise in a security's price above a resistance level (commonly its previous high price) or drop below a support level (commonly the former lowest price). A breakout is believed to indicate a continued movement in the same direction.

BREAKPOINT

A purchase of shares in an open-end mutual fund that is large enough to entitle the buyer to lower sales charges. Various breakpoints are established by the fund, at each of which the charge is reduced.

BULL

An optimistic investor who believes the market or the price of a security will rise.

BULL MARKET

A market in which prices of securities are generally rising.

BULLISH

A term used to describe rising security prices.

BUY-IN

When the seller of a security fails to deliver security for a settlement, the broker will purchase the security that was to be delivered on the open market and charge the seller's account for the losses incurred.

BUY/WRITE

An advanced option order that combines the purchase with a security and the sale of the corresponding call options.

BUYER'S OPTION (CONTRACT)

A settlement that calls for delivery and payment according to the number of days specified by the buyer.

BUYING POWER

In a margin account, the maximum amount of marginable securities that the client can purchase or sell short without having to deposit additional funds.

BUYOUT

The purchase of a controlling interest (or per cent of shares) in a company's stock.

❐

C

CALL

An option contract gives the holder of the option the rights (but not the obligation) to purchase, and obligates the writer to sell a specified number of shares of the underlying asset at the given strike price on or before the expiration date of the contract.

CALL DATE

The date when callable bonds are eligible to be redeemed before maturity.

CALL PROTECTION

The degree of security that an investor has against a bond being called, usually measured by the number of years between today and the call date.

CALL SPREAD

Simultaneously buying and selling a call options contract on the same underlying security but with different expiration dates, different exercise prices, or both.

CALLABLE

A securities feature of some bonds or convertible securities that allow the issuer to retire the issue prior to the original maturity date. If the current interest rate falls below the yield paid on the security, it is in the issuer's best interest to call and retire the security, then reissue at the new lower rate. To reflect this risk for the holder of the security, a callable security is usually priced lower than a non-callable security.

CALLABLE BOND

A bond which the issuer can decide to redeem before its stated maturity date. A call date and a call price are always given. A callable bond usually trades lower than a non-callable one.

CAPITAL EXPENDITURE

The expenditure incurred during a particular period to acquire long-term assets such as land, plant, or equipment.

CAPITAL GAIN

The amount by which an asset's selling price exceeds its original purchase price. A realised capital gain is an investment that has been sold at a profit, an unrealised capital gain is an investment that would result in a profit if sold. IRS (Internal Revenue Service) levies capital gains tax for realised capital gains from the sale of mutual funds, bonds, options, homes, and businesses.

CAPITAL GROWTH

The increase in the value of an investment when either its price rises or its profits are reinvested.

CAPITALISATION

The total value of all stocks and bonds issued by a corporation.

CAPITAL LOSS

The decrease in the value of an investment or asset; opposite of capital gain.

CAPITAL STOCK

The common and preferred stock of a corporation.

CASH FLOW

Sometimes called cash earnings, it is the net earnings before depreciation, amortisation and non-cash charges, useful in determining the solvency of a company. Cash flow is calculated by adding depreciation to net earnings and then subtracting preferred dividends.

CASH DIVIDEND

A dividend paid in cash to the shareholders of a company. This amount is usually based on profitability of the corporation and decisions of the board of directors. This is considered as a taxable income.

CASH AND EQUIVALENTS

The value of a company's assets that can be converted into cash immediately. These assets usually include bank accounts and liquid marketable securities, such as government bonds and banker's acceptances.

CERTIFICATE

An electronic or physical document representing ownership of a stock or bond.

CHANGES IN FINANCIAL POSITION

Sources of funds internally provided from operations that alter a company's cash flow position: depreciation, deferred taxes, other sources, and capital expenditures.

CHIEF EXECUTIVE OFFICER (CEO)

The highest ranking executive who manages the day-to-day operations of the corporation, as appointed by the board of directors.

CLASS

Options of the same type, calls or puts on the same security.

CLEARING CORPORATIONS

A distribution centre operated for its member brokerage firms, which works with the exchanges to streamline trade comparison, settlement and assignment procedures.

CLIENT (ACCOUNT) STATEMENT

A statement of a client's positions and activities that is required to be sent out quarterly. However, if there is monthly activity on the account, then it is to be sent out monthly.

CLIFFING

An investment strategy that organises bonds in the portfolio so that they all mature in the same year.

CLOSE

The price of a security's last transaction on a trading day.

CLOSED-END FUNDS

A mutual fund that does not offer new shares after the initial offering. Shares of the fund can only be purchased or sold on securities exchanges. Closed-end funds are actively managed by an investment professional.

CLOSING PURCHASE

A transaction in which the purchaser's intention is to reduce or eliminate a short option position. (Buy to close).

CLOSING SALE

A transaction in which the seller's intention is to reduce or eliminate his long option position. (Sell to close).

CLOSING TRANSACTION

The transaction executed to close an option contract. The holder would sell to close while the writer would buy to close.

COLLATERAL TRUST BOND

A debt instrument issued by one corporation and backed by the securities of another corporation.

COMBINATION

The option strategy involving the purchase or sale of both a put and a call on the same underlying security, but with different strike prices and/or expiration dates.

COMBINATION ORDER

An order simultaneously buying a call and selling a put, or buying a put and selling a call on the same underlying security.

COMMERCIAL PAPER

A short-term debt instrument issued by corporations. Its rate of interest is set at issuance and can be realised only if held to maturity.

COMMISSION

The fee paid to a brokerage for the execution of trades or management of an investment portfolio. Commission charges vary based upon the type of brokerage, and may be dependent upon the type of security, the number of shares traded, or the dollar value of the security.

COMMON EQUITY

The amount of shareholders' equity attributable to common stock. Common equity usually consists of the common stock at par value, capital surplus and retained earnings.

COMMON STOCK

A security issued representing ownership of a corporation. Common stockholders may vote to elect management, participate in corporate decision-making, and receive dividends.

COMPARISON

The correspondence between two brokerage firms outlining the terms of the transaction. Comparison can be through a clearing corporation or on a per-trade basis.

COMPETITIVE TENDER

A method of purchasing new issues of treasury bills, notes, and bonds in which the investor specifies the yield at which they are willing to purchase the security.

CONFIRMATION

The acknowledgement of a securities transaction providing the investor with information, such as the settlement date, terms, price and commission.

CONSENT TO LOAN AGREEMENT

An agreement margin clients are required to sign authorising the brokerage firm to lend the client's securities to itself or other firms.

CONSIDERATION

The money value of a transaction, calculated as the number of shares multiplied by the price, before adding commission.

CONSTANT DOLLAR INVESTMENT

Securities such as savings accounts and money market funds that do not fluctuate in price.

CONSUMER PRICE INDEX (CPI)

An inflationary indicator published monthly to reflect the upward price movement of a fixed basket of common goods and services.

CONTINGENT DEFERRED SALES CHARGE (CDSC)

The pricing structure that imposes a sales charge when investors exit a mutual fund.

CONTRACTUAL PLAN

A type of accumulation plan where a mutual fund investor makes a firm commitment to invest a specified amount of money over a specific period of time.

CONTROL PERSON

A director, officer or other affiliate of the issuer or a stockholder who owns at least 10% of outstanding stock.

CONTROL SECURITIES

Securities owned by a control person.

CONVERTIBLE ISSUE

A security feature that gives the issue holder the choice to convert to another issue, usually common stock. This privilege can be used only once.

CONVERTIBLE PREFERRED STOCK

Preferred stock that may be converted into common stock at specific prices or rates.

COOLING-OFF PERIOD

The period between the filing of the registration statement on a new issue with the Stock Exchange to the effective date of the offering.

CORNER A MARKET

To purchase a significant portion of the supply of a stock in order to manipulate its price.

CORPORATE BONDS

Bonds issued by corporations to raise capital.

CORPORATION/COMPANY

The most common form of business organisation, chartered by a state and given legal rights as a separate entity from its owners. Corporations are characterised by issuing shares of transferable stock, limited liability of its owners, and existence beyond the life of its owners.

COUPON

1. The detachable part of bearer stock certificates exchangeable for dividends.

2. The rate of interest on a fixed interest security; a 5% coupon means interest of 5% a year on the nominal value of the security.

COUPON YIELD

A bond's coupon payment divided by par value. Also called nominal yield.

COVER

The number of times the dividend paid out by a company is covered. Calculated by dividing the total net profit available with the company for distribution as dividend by the actual amount paid.

COVERED CALL

A short call option position where the writer sells a call option while simultaneously owning the number of shares represented by the option contracts. Covered calls can limit the risk of the writer since he/she has already purchased the deliverable security.

COVERED PUT

A put option position where the writer of the option is also short on the corresponding stock. This limits the option writer's risk because the put can be used to cover the short stock position.

CREDIT AGREEMENT

The agreement which outlines the credit arrangement between the broker and the client concerning a margin account.

CREDIT BALANCE

The funds available to a client in the cash or margin account. In a short sale, this balance is the client's liability.

CREDIT RISK

The danger that a bond issuer's ability to repay what it owes will deteriorate. This danger usually prompts bond rating firms to downgrade the credit rating of company or government that issued the bond, sending the yield of the bond higher to justify the increased risk associated with this bond.

CUMULATIVE DIVIDENDS

A feature of preferred stocks, whereby holders are still entitled to receiving dividends after a pay period has been skipped due to poor company performance; the accumulated dividends must be paid before common stockholders may receive any dividends.

CUMULATIVE PREFERRED STOCK

A feature of preferred stock that entitles the holder to later payment of dividends when they were not paid when due. The dividends accumulated must be paid before common stockholders may receive any dividends.

CURRENT ASSETS

Liquid assets that can be converted to cash within 12 months. These include cash, marketable securities, accounts receivable and inventory.

CURRENT INCOME

Regular income generated by investments (as opposed to capital growth).

CURRENT LIABILITIES

Accounting term describing obligations that must be paid within 12 months. These include accounts payable, short-term debt and interest on long-term debt.

CURRENT MATURITY

The number of years remaining until a bond matures.

CURRENT RATIO

An indicator of short-term debt-paying ability. It is determined by dividing current assets by current liabilities. The higher the ratio, the more liquid the company.

CURRENT SHARE PRICE

Most recent market price of the shares.

CURRENT YIELD

The actual yield of a bond determined by the bond's current price on the secondary market. The current yield can be calculated by dividing the coupon by the bond's current market price. For example, a bond with a $1,000 face value and a coupon of 5% purchased at $900 has a current yield of 6.56% (50/900). When the market price of a bond declines, its current yield rises. Conversely, when the market price rises, the current yield declines.

CYCLICALS

Stocks whose performance is heavily influenced by the business cycle. An example would be the agriculture industry, where sales change as seasons change.

❐

D

DATED DATE

The day on which interest starts to accrue on newly issued bonds.

DAY ORDER

An order that is open for the duration of the day it was entered, expiring at the close of that day's trading.

DAY TRADE

The buying and selling of the same security on the same day.

DEALER

An individual or entity, such as a security firm, that buys and sells security products and holds an inventory.

DEBENTURES

A common kind of corporate bond, often issued by a firm undergoing restructuring. Debentures are backed only by the credit quality or 'goodwill' of the issuer. With no collateral, these bonds carry a higher risk, and, therefore, offer a higher rate of return, when compared to bonds backed by asset.

DEBIT BALANCE

The amount of loan in a margin account.

DEBT/EQUITY RATIO

A comparison of the assets provided by creditors to the assets provided by shareholders. It is calculated by dividing long-term debt by common stockholders' equity, and serves as an indicator of financial leverage.

DECILE RANK

Performance of a mutual fund over time, rated on a scale of 1 to 10. One indicates that a mutual fund's return was in the top 10% of funds being compared, while 10 means the return was in the worst 10%.

DECLARATION DATE

The date on which a firm's directors meet and announce the date and amount of the next dividend payout.

DEED OF TRUST

The trust agreement drawn up when a corporation plans to issue bonds or other debt securities. It includes information, such as assets, interest payments, maturity dates, etc.

DEFAULT

An issuer's failure to pay interest on a debt security. Treasury securities are considered default-free.

DEFENSIVE STOCKS

Stocks whose prices stay stable when the market declines. Defensive stocks are usually those of industries that are less affected by recessions, such as stocks of food and utility companies.

DEFERRED (INCOME) TAXES

An amount allocated during the period to cover tax liabilities that have not yet been paid.

DELIVERY BALANCE ORDER (DBO)

An order issued by the clearing corporation to any firm that has delivery or sale position remaining after the day's trades are netted.

DEPOSITORY

A centralised location for keeping financial securities in dematerialised form.

DEPOSITORY TRUST COMPANY (DTC)

A corporation owned by banks and brokerage firms that holds securities, arranges for their receipt and delivery, and arranges for payments in settlement.

DEPRECIATION

Depreciation is a non-cash charge that represents the decline in the value of fixed assets due to deterioration, age, or obsolescence.

DERIVATIVE

The securities whose value is derived from or linked to an underlying stock, bond, currency or mortgage.

DERIVATIVE SECURITY

A financial security such as an option or a future, whose value is derived in part from the value of another security. For example, the price of an options contract is tied closely to the market price of the underlying stock.

DIAGONAL SPREAD

A spread of the same class of options but with different exercise prices and different expiration dates.

DIFFERENTIAL

The fraction of a point added to the purchase price or subtracted from the sale price of odd lot orders. The charge represents compensation to the dealer/specialist for executing the odd lot order.

DILUTION

Diminution in the proportion of income each share is entitled to when new shares are issued.

DIRECTOR

A corporate board member elected by stockholders to establish corporate policies, including the selection of the management team, and payments of dividends.

DISCOUNT

When the market price of a newly issued security is lower than the issue price.

DISCOUNT BOND

Bonds that are selling at a current price below its face value. Bonds sell at a discount when the coupon on the bond is lower than prevailing rates on similar investments.

DISCOUNT RATE

The interest rate at which member banks may borrow short-term funds from the Central Bank of the nation.

DISPOSABLE INCOME

Disposable income is the total amount available for both regular expenses and investment opportunities. It is calculated as the income available after taxes have been deducted.

DISTRIBUTIONS

The payments of dividends or capital gains. Funds are required to distribute gains (if any) to shareholders at least once per year.

DIVERGENCE

When two or more averages or indices move in different directions, failing to show a market trend.

DIVERSIFICATION

The process of dividing investments among a variety of securities to lower or even eliminate risk.

DIVIDENDS

A portion of a corporation's earnings paid to stockholders on a per-share basis. Preferred stock is supposed to pay a regular and prescribed dividend amount. Common stock pays varying amounts as determined by the company.

DIVIDEND REINVESTMENT

Automatic reinvestment of shareholder dividends into more shares of a company's stock. This is often done without having to pay commissions.

DIVIDEND REINVESTMENT PLAN

Automatic reinvestment of shareholder dividends in more shares of a company's stock without commission. Dividend reinvestment plans allow shareholders to accumulate capital over the long-term using cost averaging.

DIVIDEND YIELD (FUNDS)

Indicated yield represents return on a share of a mutual fund held over the past year.

DIVIDEND YIELD (STOCKS)

Indicated yield represents annual dividends divided by current stock price.

DIVIDENDS PER SHARE

Dividends paid for the past year divided by the number of common shares outstanding. The number of shares outstanding is determined by a weighted average of shares outstanding over the specified year.

DOLLAR COST AVERAGING

An investment strategy used in mutual funds by which clients invest a fixed dollar amount periodically, regardless of the performance of the fund. Since mutual funds permit the buying of fractional shares, the fixed amount will acquire more shares when the fund decreases in price, and fewer shares when the price rises.

DO-NOT-REDUCE (DNR)

An order instruction that informs the broker not to reduce the price of the order by the amount of dividends, if and when paid by the corporation.

DOUBLE TAXATION

Corporations pay taxes on revenue before paying dividends, then shareholders pay taxes again as dividends are considered taxable income; hence, the term "double" taxation.

DOWNGRADE

A negative change in the ratings for a rated security.

DOWNTICK

A listed equity trade whose price is lower than that of the last different sale.

DRAG ON RETURNS (DRAG GRADE)

The negative impact on returns from sales charges, annual expenses and portfolio turnover.

DUE DILIGENCE (MEETING)

The meeting between corporate officials and underwriters prior to the issuance of the security. During these meetings, contents of the prospectus are thoroughly discussed to ensure accuracy.

DURATION

The length of time it will take to recoup the principal of the investment, used to measure part of the risk in a bond or bond fund. Duration tells you how long it will take to recoup your principal. If a bond or a bond fund has a duration of 6 years, a 1% drop in interest rates will raise its value by 6%, while a 1% rise in interest rates will lower its price by 6%.

❒

E

EARNINGS

The net income for a company during the reporting period.

EARNINGS BEFORE INTEREST AND TAXES (EBIT)

A measure of a firm's earnings performance that is not clouded by debt payments or tax regulations. It is calculated as revenues minus the cost of goods sold and selling, and general expenses.

EARNINGS BEFORE INTEREST, TAXES, DEPRECIATION AND AMORTISATION (EBITDA)

Also known as operating cash flow, EBITDA is calculated by subtracting cost of sales and operating expenses from revenues. As the name implies, EBITDA does not take into consideration the interests, taxes, depreciation and amortisation costs.

EARNINGS GROWTH %

A weighted average of the one-year earnings growth rates of the stocks in the fund. This calculation excludes stocks whose earnings changed from a loss to a gain and stocks whose earnings gains exceeded 999.99%.

EARNINGS PER SHARE (EPS)

The net income divided by the number of shares of common stock outstanding.

EARNINGS REPORT

A corporate financial statement released by the company quarterly or annually netting all earnings and expenses to a profit or loss.

EARNINGS YIELD

The ratio of earnings per share to the current share price, after allowing for tax and interest payments on fixed interest debt. It is calculated by taking the total twelve months' earnings divided by the number of outstanding shares, divided by the recent price, multiplied by 100.

ECN

Electronic Communication Network. The electronic system that matches buyers and sellers for the electronic execution of trades. The benefits an investor gets from trading with an ECN include after-hours trading, avoiding market makers (and their spreads), and anonymity (which is often important for large trades).

EFFECTIVE DATE

The first date after the cooling-off period of a new issue on which the security can be offered.

ENDORSEMENT

A signature on the back of a negotiable instrument such as a stock certificate or cheque, matching the name that appears on the face, making the document negotiable.

EQUIPMENT TRUST BONDS

Debt instruments issued by some corporations that are backed by equipment, such as airplanes, locomotives or freight cars.

EQUITY

The value of the common stockholders' ownership interest in a company, in the form of common or preferred stock.

EQUITY-INCOME FUNDS

Mutual funds that focus on large company stocks that pay big dividends.

EQUITY OPTIONS

An options contract that gives the holder the right to buy or sell a specified number of shares of stock at a specified price before in a specific time period. One option usually equals 100 shares of stock.

ESTIMATED EPS GROWTH

The mean estimate of earnings-per-share growth from the estimation by market experts.

EUROPEAN-STYLE OPTION

An option contract that can only be exercised on the expiration date.

EXCHANGE

The marketplace where stocks, bonds, options, futures and commodities are traded. Major stock exchanges are: New York Stock Exchange (NYSE), NASDAQ, London Stock Exchange.

EXCHANGE-TRADED FUND (ETF)

A type of fund that tracks an index or gold, but can be traded like a stock.

EX-DIVIDEND DATE

1. The day on which the price of a security is reduced to reflect dividend payout.
2. The first day on which the buyer of a security will no longer be entitled to receive the recently announced dividend payment.

EXECUTION

The completion of a securities trade.

EXERCISE

To utilise the right of the options holder to buy (call option) or sell (put option) the underlying security.

EXERCISE PRICE

The stated price per share at which the underlying asset may be traded between the holder and writer of the options contract. Also called strike price.

EXPENSE RATIO

The operating costs, management fees, administrative fees and all other costs incurred by the fund expressed as a percentage of the fund's total asset.

EXPIRATION

The day on which an option contract becomes void.

EXPIRATION CYCLE

The cycle of 3 months on which options on a particular security expire. Options are placed in one of the three cycles: the January cycle (January, April, July, October), the February cycle (February, May, August, November), or the March cycle (March, June, September, December).

EXPIRATION DATE

The last day on which an option may be exercised for American-style options. For European options, this is the only date when the option can be exercised.

EXPIRATION MONTH

The month when an option or futures contract expires.

EX-RIGHTS DATE

The date after which stocks are traded without subscription rights.

EXTENDED MATURITY

A provision whereby a bond continues to pay interest after the stated maturity.

EX-WARRANTS DATE

The date after which stocks traded are not entitled to warrants which are to be distributed.

❐

F

FAST MARKET

A market condition where a large number of orders for a particular security are received within a short period of time, faster than what market makers can handle effectively. These situations are usually the results of unexpected news and may lead to price volatility.

FILL OR KILL (FOK)

An order instruction requesting the immediate execution of the entire order quantity at the specified price. If not, then the order is automatically cancelled.

FISCAL AGENT

The authority responsible for issuing new agency securities.

FISCAL YEAR

The twelve-month period during which businesses or the government maintain financial records. This cycle does not necessarily coincide with the calendar year. Therefore, it is known as the fiscal year.

FIXED ANNUITY

Guaranteed payments of a specified fixed dollar amount annually for the period covered under the contract.

FLAT

A security position that is neither long nor short in a portfolio.

FLAT (BONDS)

A bond trading without accrued interest is said to be trading "flat".

FLOOR BROKER

An exchange member permitted to conduct business on the exchange floor.

FLOTATION

A company's shares offered on the market for the first time.

FRACTIONAL SHARES

A share of equity that is less than one full share. Fractional shares usually come about from stock splits, dividend reinvestment plans (DRIPs) and similar corporate actions. Normally, fractional shares cannot be acquired from the market.

FREE CASH FLOW

Free cash flow is calculated as operating cash flow minus capital expenditures and dividends. Free cash flow can be used to pay dividends, buy back stock or pay-off debt.

FREE CASH FLOW PER SHARE

Free cash flow divided by the number of common shares outstanding.

FREE STOCK

The securities that can be used for a loan.

FRIENDLY TAKEOVER

A takeover supported by the target company's management and board members.

FROZEN ACCOUNT

An account that had failed to make timely payments in the past, thereby requires all purchases to be paid for in cash in advance for a period of 90 days.

FULLY DILUTED EARNINGS PER SHARE

Earnings per share expressed as though all outstanding convertible securities and warrants have been exercised.

FULLY DILUTED SHARES OUTSTANDING

All shares outstanding, including common stock, warrants, and convertible securities.

FULLY PAID SECURITIES LENDING

A strategy used by investors to generate additional income in their portfolios. Securities lending is when an individual temporarily lends fully paid securities to a financial institution (the borrower). The transaction is usually facilitated by an intermediary, like a clearing firm. All parties enter into a lending agreement (Master Securities Lending Agreement) that covers the rights of all counter-parties and governs all transactions.

FUND EXCHANGE

Ability to shift a mutual fund investment from one fund to another within same mutual fund family.

FUND FAMILY

The group of mutual funds managed by a single company.

FUNDAMENTAL ANALYSIS

The security valuation method involving the analysis of the company's financials and operations, especially sales, earnings, growth potential, assets/debt ratio, management, and competition. This valuation method seeks to find the intrinsic value of a company, and locate undervalued stock in the market.

FUTURES

An agreement to buy or sell a set amount of a commodity or financial instrument at a certain price on a predetermined date.

FUTURES CONTRACT

Agreement to buy or sell a set number of shares of a specific stock in a predetermined future month at a price agreed upon by both sides of the transaction. The contracts themselves are traded on the futures market. The difference between a futures contract and an options contract is that the futures contract is an agreement to actually make a transaction, whereas the option contract is the right to buy or sell.

❐

G

GEARING

A company's debt expressed as a percentage of its equity capital.

GENERAL OBLIGATION (GO) BOND

A municipal bond backed by the full taxing power of the issuing municipality.

GOOD DELIVERY

Securities delivered to the broker from the seller, properly endorsed to be delivered to the buyer.

GOOD-TILL-CANCELLED (GTC)

An order that remains open until it is either executed or cancelled.

GOODWILL

The intangible asset of a company, such as a strong brand name or reputation.

GOVERNMENT BOND

Debt security issued by the State or Central Government of a country.

GROSS PROFIT

The net sales before tax minus cost of sales.

GROWTH AND INCOME FUNDS

Mutual funds that invest in companies whose earnings are expected to grow, sacrificing some future profits in order to provide current income.

GROWTH STOCK

Stock of a company in an emerging young industry.

❐

H

HEAD AND SHOULDERS

A technical analysis term, describing the chart formation where a stock price peak is preceded and followed by two smaller peaks, both at the resistance point of a stock cycle. This formation sometimes indicates a trend reversal. The name is derived from the similarity in appearance to the human head and shoulders.

HEDGE

To reduce the risk in one security by taking an offsetting position in a related security.

HIGH-YIELD BOND

A high-yield bond is one that is rated poorly by a credit rating system. These bonds offer higher yields compared to bonds of financially sound companies, justifying the greater credit risk.

HOLDING COMPANY

A corporation that owns enough voting stock in another firm and influences the election of its board of directors, gaining control of the management and operations.

HOSTILE TAKEOVER

A takeover against the will of the target company's management and board members.

HOUSE MAINTENANCE CALL

The brokerage firm requesting the client for additional funds because the equity in the client's margin account has fallen below the minimum amount set by the brokerage.

HOUSE REQUIREMENT

The minimum amount of equity brokerage firms require margin clients to maintain in the account; failure to meet this would result in a House Maintenance Call.

HYPOTHECATION

A pledging of assets as collateral necessary to secure a debit balance in a margin account.

❐

I

IMMEDIATE-OR-CANCEL (IOC)

An order instructing for execution at the stated price for as many shares as can be filled immediately, the unfilled remaining amount will be cancelled.

INCOME

The portion of investment return from interest or dividend payments, taxable at an individual's ordinary income tax rate.

INCOME BONDS

Bonds issued by a corporation in poor financial condition, interest is paid only if earned by the issuer. These bonds are speculative instruments that pay high rates of interest for its high risks.

INCOME FUNDS

Funds that focus on a variety of securities that earn high interests or dividends.

INCOME STOCK

Common stock that pays an unusually high dividend.

INCOME STREAM

A strategy arranging bonds so that they produce a consistent series of payments.

INDENTURE

The terms and agreement of a corporate bond, usually on the face of the bond certificate.

INDEX FUND

A mutual fund whose portfolio matches that of an index, such as the S&P 500 or Nifty. This allows the fund to reflect the performance of the overall market.

INDICATED DIVIDEND

An estimate of the dividend per share that would be paid over the next 12 months if each dividend were the same amount as the most recent dividend.

INDICATED YIELD

The yield based on the annualised value of the most recent dividend, calculated by dividing the annual dividend by the price of the stock.

INDUSTRY

A category describing a company's primary business activity. This is usually determined by the corporation's largest source of revenue.

INFLATION

The rate at which the general level of prices for goods and services is rising, usually measured by the Consumer Price Index or Producer Price Index.

INFLATION RISK

The risk that the yield of an investment will be diminished by rising inflation rates.

INITIAL INVESTMENT

The amount required to make the first investment in a mutual fund.

INITIAL PUBLIC OFFERING (IPO)

A company's first sale of stock to the public, usually by a young company to capitalise for further expansion and growth.

INSIDE INFORMATION

Relevant information about a company that has not yet been made public. It is illegal to execute or make trades based on this information.

INSIDER

A person with non-public information on a corporation. Directors and officers who have access to non-public information before the public are usually considered insiders.

INSIDER TRADING

The illegal purchase or sale of shares by someone who possesses inside information about the company. For example, an executive who purchases shares with knowledge of a new invention soon to be announced by his company would be performing illegal insider trading.

INSTITUTIONAL INVESTOR

Entities with large amounts of funds to invest, such as investment companies, mutual funds, brokerages, insurance companies, and endowment funds. Institutional investors account for the majority of overall market volume.

INTEREST

The rate charged by the lender for borrowing money over a specified amount of time.

INTEREST COVERAGE

The ratio measuring a firm's ability to pay interest on its debt, calculated by dividing net earnings before interest and taxes by the interest expense on bonds and other long-term debt. Higher ratio means a lower possibility of default.

INTEREST EXPENSE

The interest paid out by a corporation for loans and debt securities issued.

INTEREST RATE

The rate charged by a lender for borrowing money.

Interest rates are generally fixed at a certain level for the entire length of a loan, though they can also vary over time.

INTEREST RATE RISK

The risk that prevailing interest rates will rise above the rate on the fixed income securities you are holding, resulting in a decline of the security's price. The longer the life of the bond, the greater the interest rate risks.

INTERIM DIVIDEND

A dividend declared and distributed part way through a company's financial year, before annual earnings have been calculated, authorised solely by the directors.

INTERMEDIATE-TERM BONDS

Bonds with maturities of four to ten years.

INTERNATIONAL FUNDS

Mutual funds that invest in foreign companies.

INTERNAL RATE OF RETURN (IRR)

Internal rate of return (IRR) is a metric used in capital budgeting measuring the profitability. Internal rate of return (IRR) is a metric used in capital budgeting measuring the profitability of potential investments.

IN-THE-MONEY

An option is in-the-money when holder would profit from exercising the contract. For example, a call option is in-the-money, if the exercise price is less than the market price of the underlying security, and a put option is in-the-money, if the strike price is greater than the market price of the underlying security.

INVENTORY

The monetary value of a company's raw materials, work in process, supplies used in operations and finished goods. Excess inventory on the balance sheet can represent slowdowns in sales or overproduction. Inventory is considered liquid assets, since they can be easily converted into cash.

INVESTMENT ADVISOR

The individual or firm responsible for managing a portfolio or mutual fund.

ISSUE

A security offered for sale by a government or corporation.

ISSUE DATE

The date when a security was initially issued.

ISSUED STOCK

Stock sold to the public.

❐

J

JOINT ACCOUNT

An account with two or more individuals acting as co-owners.

JUNK BOND

Bonds rated with the lowest credit rating, usually issued by companies in financial turmoil. Since they are riskier, they offer a much higher yield.

❐

L

LADDER

A portfolio strategy where an investor creates a portfolio consisting of various fixed income securities that are approximately the same value, but each with different lengths until maturity. This helps reduce interest rate risk.

LARGE-CAP STOCKS

Stocks issued by companies that are valued at high market capitalization. Each country has different slaps to declare a company as a large-cap.

LAST

The price at which the security was last traded.

LIABILITY

An obligation to a pay debt owed, or to fulfil a duty or responsibility.

LIMIT ORDER

An order instruction which sets the highest price the client is willing to pay for a buy order, or the lowest price the client is willing to accept for a sell order. If the security reaches the price specified by the limit order, the order will be executed at the specified price or possibly better.

LIMITED TAX BOND

A municipal bond whose ability to pay back principal and interest is based on a special tax.

LIMITED TRADING AUTHORISATION

An account where the client gives the power to make trades in his account to another person.

LIQUIDATION

1. Closing out a position, converting assets into cash.
2. Action taken by margin department when a client has not paid for a purchase.

LIQUIDITY

The degree of ease to convert an asset into cash.

LIQUIDITY RATIO

A measure of how much dollar volume is required to move the stock's price up or down one percentage point. A high ratio indicates that relatively heavy trading is required to change its price, while a low liquidity ratio indicates that the stock moves on relatively light volume.

LIQUIDITY RISK

Risk from the difficulty in selling an asset. High liquidity risk could lower the value of the asset.

LISTED OPTIONS

Options that are traded on a national option exchange.

LISTED SECURITIES

Securities that are traded on a stock exchange.

LISTED STOCK

Stock that has met the qualifications for trading on an exchange.

LOAD

The sales charge assessed upon the initial investment in or redemption of a mutual fund.

LOAD FUND

A mutual fund with shares sold at a price including a sales charge, usually purchased through a salesperson.

LOAN STOCK

A stock bearing a fixed rate of interest. Unlike a debenture, loan stocks may be unsecured.

LOAN VALUE

The amount of money the client may borrow from the firm, expressed as a percentage of market value.

LONG POSITION

The state of an investor owning a security.

LONG-TERM ASSETS

Value of long-term property, equipment and other capital assets minus the depreciation over time.

LONG-TERM BOND

Bonds that mature in more than ten years.

LONG-TERM DEBT

Liabilities to be paid after 12 months from the date of the last balance sheet.

LONG-TERM DEBT/CAPITALISATION

The ratio of long-term debt as a proportion of the capital available, serves as an indicator of financial leverage. Calculated by dividing long-term debt with the sum of long-term debt, preferred stock and common stockholders' equity.

LONG-TERM LIABILITIES

Amount owed for interests, bond repayment, and other debt that are due after one year.

LOW

The lowest closing price of a stock over a certain period of time.

❑

N

NAKED CALL

An investor selling a call options contract without actually owning the underlying security.

NEGOTIABLE

A feature of a security enabling the owner to transfer title or ownership.

NET ASSETS

The total assets held in a mutual fund.

NET ASSET VALUE

The value of a fund's assets divided by the number of its outstanding shares.

NET EARNINGS (NET INCOME)

Also known as the bottom line, this is the profit a company realises after all costs, expenses and taxes have been paid. It is calculated by subtracting business, depreciation, interest and tax costs from revenues. Also called net income or net profit.

NET MARGIN

A measure of company profitability after deducting all costs, expenses and taxes. It is calculated by dividing net earnings by revenues, the resulting percentage is the operating efficiency of a company.

NEW ISSUE

A company issuing security to the market for the first time or issuing additional shares.

NIL PAID

A new issue of shares dealt on the stock market on which no payment has yet been made, usually from a new issue or rights issue.

NO-LOAD

Without any sales commissions.

NO-LOAD FUND

An open-end fund purchased directly from a fund company or brokerage firm at the fund's net asset value, without charges to purchase or redeem shares.

NOISE

Price and volume fluctuations that do not show a clear market direction.

NOMINAL YIELD

The interest rate stated on the face of the bond.

NOMINEE NAME

Name in which a security is registered and held on behalf of the beneficial owner.

NON-CALLABLE

A note or bond that cannot be called before maturity.

NON-COMPETITIVE TENDER

The purchase of treasury bills, notes, and bonds directly from the Central Bank at the average price of accepted competitive bids during an auction of new securities.

NON-CUMULATIVE PREFERRED STOCK

The type of preferred stock that does not pay accrued dividends to its holders.

NOTE

The general name for agency security with a maturity of less than 10 years.

NTF

Stands for "No-Transaction-Fee", describes mutual funds that don't charge a transaction fee.

❐

O

OBJECTIVE (MUTUAL FUND)

The investment strategy of a mutual fund as stated in the prospectus.

ODD LOT

A quantity of securities smaller than 100 shares, which is considered the standard unit of trading.

OFFER

The lowest price at which an investor or dealer is willing to sell shares of a security.

OFFER PRICE (MUTUAL FUND)

The purchase price of a load fund, calculated by adding the fund's sales charges to its net asset value.

ON-BALANCE VOLUME INDEX

This is the ratio of volume to upward price movement, used in technical analysis to determine if a security is being heavily bought into or sold out of.

OPEN-END FUND

A mutual fund that continuously offers shares and stands ready to buy any shares redeemed by the shareholders.

OPEN-END MANAGEMENT COMPANY

A management company that constantly issues new shares.

OPEN INTEREST

The number of outstanding option contracts for a particular class or series currently in the exchange market.

OPEN OUTCRY SYSTEM

The public auction in trading pits of exchanges that involve verbal bids and offers.

OPENING PURCHASE

A transaction made by an investor with the intention of creating or increasing a long option position.

OPENING SALE

A transaction made by an investor with the intention of creating or increasing a short option position.

OPENING TRANSACTION

An investor either buying or selling an option contract to open a new position.

OPERATING MARGIN

A company's profitability before non-cash charges, it is

a measure of a company's operating efficiency. Operating margin is calculated by dividing EBITDA by revenues, then multiplying by 100.

OPTION

A contract that gives the buyer the right to buy (call) or sell (put) a predetermined quantity of an underlying security during a specific period of time at a predetermined price.

OPTION ADJUSTMENTS

Adjustments made to the terms of an option contract to reflect changes in the underlying security, such as a dividend payment or split.

OPTION AGREEMENT

The agreement the client must sign to trade options.

OPTION CLASS

The group of options with the same underlying security.

OPTION INCOME FUND

A mutual fund which tries to generate additional income by continuously writing options.

OPTION SERIES

The groups of options that have same strike price, expiration date, and unit of trading on the same underlying stock.

ORDER BOOK OFFICIAL

An employee of an exchange who maintains a book of public orders and executes limit orders on behalf of the membership.

ORDINARY SHARES

The most common form of shares, also known as common stock.

ORIGINAL ISSUE DISCOUNT (OID)

The discount from par value when the bond is first issued.

ORIGINAL ISSUE ZEROS

Zero-coupon securities that were originally issued by a corporation or government as a zero-coupon bond, instead of by severing interest and principal payments from an existing bond.

OTC BULLETIN BOARD

An electronic service that provides selected quotes on over-the-counter stocks.

OTHER CURRENT ASSETS

Accounting term describing the value of non-cash assets, including prepaid expenses and accounts receivable due within the year.

OUT-OF-THE-MONEY

An option is out-of-the-money if the price of the underlying security is below the strike price of a call option, or above that of a put. The holder would suffer an immediate loss if he was to exercise the right and purchase or sale the underlying security.

OVERBOUGHT/OVERSOLD INDICATOR

An indicator which attempts to define when prices have moved too rapidly in either direction and, thus, are vulnerable to reaction.

OVER-THE-COUNTER MARKET (OTC)

Comprises a network of telephone and telecommunication systems over which unlisted securities and other issues trade.

❒

P

PAR VALUE

The face value of a bond.

PARTICIPATING PREFERRED

A type of preferred stock giving holders the right to "participate" in any dividend payouts for common stock over and above those normally paid to common and preferred stockholders.

PASS-THROUGH SECURITY

Instrument representing an interest in a pool of mortgages, paying interest and principal on a monthly basis.

PAYEE

The person or business receiving a payment.

PAYMENT DATE

The date on which an announced stock dividend or a bond interest payment is to be made.

PAYOUT RATIO

The per cent of earnings-per-share that was paid out as dividend, calculated by dividing the quarterly dividend by the quarterly EPS, then multiplying by 100.

PEG RATIO

The price-to-earnings-growth ratio is used to find companies that are trading at a discount to the potential future growth. It is calculated by dividing a stock's forward P/E by its projected three-to five-year annual EPS growth rate. Lower PEG ratios represent a better value, since the investor would be paying less for future earnings growth.

PENNY STOCKS

Securities priced at a very low price, often highly speculative investments.

PER CENT IN TOP FIVE HOLDINGS

Proportion of total assets in the fund's largest five positions.

PHANTOM INTEREST

The interest accreted annually from a zero-coupon security, even though payment of interest is not made until the zero matures.

PIN

A personal identification number, designed for secure access into an account for the account-holder only.

PIT

The circular area on a trading floor, where futures and options are bought and sold.

PIVOT

A price level noted by the market's failure to penetrate or a sudden increase in volume that accompanies the move through the price level.

POINT

A price movement of one full increment.

POINT AND FIGURE CHART

A chart that only displays whole integer changes in price, disregarding the element of time.

PORTFOLIO

An investor's combined investment holdings, including cash, stocks, bonds, mutual funds and real estate.

PORTFOLIO TURNOVER

A measure of the portfolio trading activity for a mutual fund, calculated by dividing the lesser of purchases or sales by the average total asset value for the year.

POSITION LIMITS

The maximum number of option contracts of a particular listed security that may be held by an investor.

PRE-EMPTIVE RIGHT

An opportunity for current shareholders to maintain their percentage of ownership if additional shares of the same class are issued. The pre-emptive right allows them to purchase new shares at a specific price.

PREFERRED STOCK

Stock that represents ownership in the issuing corporation, with a specific dividend which accumulates if not paid. In the case of bankruptcy, preferred stock has a claim on assets ahead of common stockholders but after debentures.

PREMIUM (BONDS)

A bond selling at a current market price that is above its face value. Bonds sell at a premium when the coupon on the bond is higher than the prevailing rates.

PREMIUM (OPTIONS)

The price paid by the buyer to the option writer for the rights to the option contract.

PRE-TAX MARGIN

The profitability of a company before paying taxes, calculated by dividing pre-tax earnings by revenues.

PRICE/BOOK

The ratio of a stock's latest closing price divided by its book value per share. Book value per share is obtained by dividing the book value (total assets minus total liabilities) by total shares outstanding.

PRICE/CASH FLOW

The ratio of a stock's latest closing price divided by cash flow per share of the last 12 months.

PRICE/EARNINGS RATIO

The ratio obtained by dividing the current share price by the latest earnings per share.

PRICE/SALES

The ratio of a stock's latest closing price divided by revenue per share. Since this ratio reveals little about the profitability of a company, it is usually used for companies with no earnings, since those companies have an undefined P/E ratio.

PRICE SPREAD

A simultaneous purchase and sale of two options with the same expiration date but different exercise prices.

PRICE-WEIGHTED INDEX

An index calculated by adding together stock prices to compute a figure that indicates the general condition of the market, such as the Dow Jones Index.

PRIMARY DEALER

An institution recognised by the treasury department as eligible to bid on treasuries when they are initially issued and to make a market for secondary buyers.

PRIMARY MARKET

The market for new securities purchased directly from the issuer.

PRINCIPAL

The role played by a brokerage firm when it acts as a dealer, trading securities for its own account.

PRINCIPAL (BOND)

The face value of a bond.

PRIVATE COMPANY

A company where all ownership is held privately.

PRIVATE PLACEMENT

An issue offered to selected investors as opposed to being publicly offered.

PRIVATISATION

Conversion of a state-run company to a public limited company by selling its shares to the public.

PROFIT MARGIN

An indicator of profitability, calculated by dividing net income by revenue for a specific period.

PROGRAM TRADING

Trades entered into a computer program to be executed automatically.

PROSPECTUS

A detailed document for a new security issue explaining the terms, issuer, officers, public accounting firms, legal opinion, and core business. Required by any of the security regulations to be made available to any client who purchases the issues.

PROXY

Document transferring of the shareholder's voting rights, usually to a member of the company's management, to represent the shareholder's interests at a shareholder meeting.

PROXY FIGHT

An attempt by a dissident group to take over the management of a corporation, sending proxies and electing them to the board while the current management sends proxies favouring themselves. Shareholders vote between one proxy and the other.

PUBLIC MARKET

The listed exchanges through which zero-coupon investments can be purchased and sold.

PUBLIC OFFERING DATE

The first day new security issues are offered to the public.

PURCHASE PRICE

The price paid for the purchase of a treasury or agency security.

PUT

An option contract that gives the holder the right to sell a stated number of shares of the underlying security at a specified strike price to the writer of the put, up to the expiration date.

❐

Q

QUARTERLY REFUNDING

Auctions of treasury notes and bonds occurring in May, August, November and February.

QUARTERLY REPORT

An unaudited financial report submitted every quarter to the SEC by public companies, containing the company's financials and other relevant information.

QUICK RATIO

Also known as acid test, it is an indicator of a company's financial condition, calculated by taking current assets, less inventories, then divided by current liabilities.

QUOTE

The highest bid and the lowest asking price for a security at a particular time.

❐

R

R-SQUARED

A measure of how closely a fund's performance is correlated to a market index. It is calculated by comparing monthly returns over the past three years to those of a benchmark. A higher value for r-square represents a higher correlation to the performance of the overall market.

RANGE

The difference between the high and low trading prices during a given period.

RATE OF RETURN

The percentage gain or loss within a specific time period, assuming that all distributions are reinvested at the current rate of return.

RATING

The alphabetical evaluation of a bond's investment quality.

REAL-TIME QUOTE

A stock or bond quote that shows a security's most recent ask and bid prices.

REALISED GAINS/LOSSES

The gain or loss that is realised after converting the security into cash.

RECORD DATE

A date established by a corporation's board of directors, marking when a shareholder must own shares in order to receive a dividend.

REDEMPTION

The retiring of a debt instrument by repaying the principal balance to the investors.

REDEMPTION (MUTUAL FUND)

The withdrawal of assets from a mutual fund.

REDEMPTION DATE

The date on which a fixed-income security is due to be repaid by the issuer at face value.

REDEMPTION FEE

The fee applied when assets are withdrawn from a mutual fund before a specified time period, usually 60 to 90 days after the initial investment in the fund.

REDEMPTION NOTICE

A notice that the issuer of a security is calling or redeeming the issue.

REFUNDING

The retiring of a debt instrument using proceeds from the issuance of a new debt instrument.

REGISTERED BOND

A bond with owner's name, which appears on the certificate.

REGISTERED FORM

The record of security ownership on the issuer's central ledger.

REGISTERED TO PRINCIPAL ONLY

A feature of a bond whose ownership is registered with the issuer's central ledger. Interest payments are made only when coupons are clipped off and cashed in.

REGISTERED TRADER

A member of an exchange responsible for adding liquidity to the marketplace through the purchase and sale of assigned securities from his own inventory.

REGISTRAR

A commercial bank or trust company that maintains a registry of share owners and the number of shares held.

REGISTRATION STATEMENT

Carefully prepared documents, including a prospectus, filed with the Securities and Exchange Commission explaining an impending issue and pertinent data about the issuer.

REGULAR WAY

Settlement on the third business day following the date of the trade.

REINVESTMENT OPPORTUNITY

The opportunity to reinvest interest and principal paid by income securities.

REINVESTMENT RATE

The rate of interest that can be earned by reinvesting the interest payments.

REINVESTMENT RISK

The risk that securities might not be able to pay higher rates when prevailing interest rates rise, or retain previous rates when the prevailing rates decline.

RELATIVE STRENGTH

A comparison between a stock's price movement over the past year and the movement of the benchmark index in the same time period.

RESISTANCE (RESISTANCE LEVEL)

The inability of a stock to rise above a certain price.

RESTRICTED ACCOUNT

A margin account in which the debit balance exceeds the loan value.

RESTRICTED SECURITIES

Unregistered securities with limited transferability, usually acquired in a private placement.

RETAINED EARNINGS

The portion of earnings not paid out as dividends, but are instead retained by the firm for reinvestments.

RETRACEMENT

A price movement in the opposite direction of the previous trend.

RETURN

The money earned by investments over a period of time.

RETURN ON ASSETS (ROA)

A measure of a company's profitability, calculated by dividing the net income from the past fiscal year earnings by total assets, not taking into account the company's liabilities.

RETURN ON EQUITY (ROE)

An indicator of a company's profitability, calculated by dividing net income from the past fiscal year by shareholders' equity, showing how efficiently the company uses shareholders' money.

REVENUES

The total amount a company makes selling its products and/or services.

REVENUE BOND

A municipal bond whose issuer's ability to pay interest and principal is based on the revenue earned from the specific project financed by the bond.

REVERSE STOCK SPLIT

A plan instituted by a corporation to proportionally reduce the number of shares outstanding while maintaining the value of shares held by shareholders. This can boost the price of the stock higher, make it more attractive to risk-averse investors.

RIGHT

A certificate showing an existing stockholder has the privilege of purchasing new securities in proportion to the number of shares already owned before the general public, thereby maintaining his ownership percentage in the company.

RIGHTS ARBITRAGE

A simultaneous purchase and sale of different securities in anticipation of a merger or tender offer.

RIGHTS ISSUE

An offer to existing shareholders, giving them the opportunity to purchase additional shares in the company.

RIGHTS OFFERING

An offer to existing shareholders, giving them rights to buy newly issued shares at a discount from the price at which shares will later be offered to the public.

RISK

The inherent possibility that an investment will lose value.

RISK/RETURN TRADE-OFF

The relationship between the risk and return of investments. Higher risk is usually justified by higher returns, while a less risky investment will have a relatively lower rate.

ROADSHOW

Prior to a company's security offering, bankers and company management travel to present their company to potential investors with the purpose of generating interest in the issue to set a favourable price.

❐

S

SALES CHARGE/LOAD

The fee investors must pay to buy shares in a mutual fund, either paid when shares are purchased or withdrawn. Also known as load.

SAME-DAY SUBSTITUTION

Purchasing one security and selling another of near equal value on the same day.

SAVINGS BONDS

A registered, non-callable, non-negotiable bond sold at a discount, redeemable at face value upon maturity.

SECONDARY MARKET

The market where securities are traded after the initial offering.

SECONDARY OFFERINGS

A company selling additional stock to the market after its initial offering, attempting to raise additional capital.

SECTOR FUNDS

Mutual funds that focus on investing in a specific industry; these funds have higher risks because of their lack of diversity.

SECURITIES

The general term used to describe investment products, including any stock, treasury stock, bond, debenture, etc. Excludes fixed annuities and insurance policies.

SELL OUT

When client incurs a margin or maintenance call and fails to settle the balance by settlement date, the brokerage will sell the securities at the best price available, and hold the client liable for the price and costs.

SELL/WRITE

An advanced option strategy that combines the short selling of a stock and the simultaneous selling of a put option on the same underlying stock.

SERIAL BONDS

An issue of bonds that matures over a period of years.

SERIES

All option contracts of the same class which have the same unit of trade, expiration date, and strike price.

SETTLEMENT

The payment and delivery of securities after a trade.

SETTLEMENT DATE

The date on which security transactions are settled. Settlement is generally three business days after the trade.

SETTLEMENT DATE INVENTORY

The total of all positions in a security on settlement date.

SHAREHOLDER

A person or entity that owns shares in a corporation.

SHAREHOLDERS' EQUITY

The difference between a company's total assets and total liabilities. Sometimes called net worth or book value, shareholders' equity represents the shareholders' ownership of the company. See Price/Book Ratio.

SHAREHOLDER SERVICES FEE

A fee that the mutual fund pays to the fund's sponsor to provide for the sponsor's administrative services.

SHARES OUTSTANDING

Shares of common stock that are currently owned by investors.

SHARE REPURCHASE

A program by which a corporation buys back some

of its own shares in the open market, reducing the shares outstanding and, thus, increases earnings and dividends per share, driving up the stock price.

SHORT ACCOUNT

The margin account in which the client has sold short securities.

SHORT EXEMPT

Type of short sale order that can be executed during a decrease, or downtick, in the price of the stock.

SHORT INTEREST

A technical analysis of market sentiment, calculated by dividing the total shares sold short of a stock by its average daily trading volume.

SHORT POSITION

A technique used by investors who believe the price of a stock is going down, selling stocks they do not yet own, then later buying it back at a lower price to close out the transaction.

SHORT SELL

The sale of securities that are not owned with the intention to buy it back at a later date at a lower price.

SHORT-TERM BOND

A bond that matures within five years.

SHORT-TERM BOND FUNDS

Funds that invest in bonds with average maturities of three years or less.

SHORT-TERM GOVERNMENT BOND

A government bond that matures within five years.

SIZE

The number of shares available at a given quote.

SLIPPAGE

The difference between estimated transaction costs and actual transaction costs.

SMALL CAP STOCKS

Stocks issued by companies that are valued at less than the slab set by stock exchange. Small cap stocks can offer high growth opportunities, but are more risky and pay little dividends; if not, none at all.

SMALL COMPANY FUNDS

Funds that invest in companies with a market cap of $500 million or less.

SPECIAL-PURPOSE BOND

Municipal bond which is repaid from taxes collected from those who benefit from the project the bond's proceeds were used to finance.

SPECIALIST

A member of an exchange who makes a market in certain traded securities.

SPIN-OFF

Selling off a part of an existing firm to form another independent company, through the sale or distribution of new shares.

SPLIT FUND

A mutual fund that holds treasury securities and other types of investments.

SPONSOR

The organiser of a fund, usually also the initial shareholder.

SPREAD

The difference between the bid and ask of a quote.

SPREAD ORDER

An advanced options strategy that involves the combined purchase and sale of two puts or two calls on the same underlying security.

STANDARD DEVIATION

A statistical term describing the variations from the average; it measures a fund's or portfolio's historical volatility by looking at the past returns. The higher the standard deviation, the greater the potential for volatility.

STATEMENT OF ADDITIONAL INFORMATION

A document containing additional detailed information not included in a mutual fund's prospectus. It can be obtained by request to the fund company.

STATEMENT OF CASH FLOWS

A financial statement showing a firm's cash transactions during a specified period.

STOCK

A share in the ownership of a company, representing a proportionate claim to the company's earnings and assets.

STOCK AHEAD

Refers to a limit order that has not been executed because of other orders at the same limit that were entered earlier.

STOCK DIVIDEND

Payment of dividends in the form of stock rather than cash. The stock could be additional shares of the same company or that of a spun-off subsidiary.

STOCK POWER

A power of attorney enabling a person other than the owner to transfer stock ownwership to another party.

STOCK SPLITS

The exchange of existing shares for more newly issued

shares from the same corporation. Splits do not increase or decrease the capitalisation of the company; shareholders' equity is simply redistributed over more shares, making the price of each individual share cheaper.

STOP LIMIT ORDER

Similar to a stop order, but instead of becoming a market order, when the price is reached or passed, it becomes a limit order at the specified price.

STOP-LOSS

An automatic order to sell an instrument, once its price reaches a specified level, mostly used for volatile stocks, so that potential losses are limited if the stock declines rapidly.

STOP ORDER

A type of order not executed until the specified price has been reached or passed, at which it becomes a market order. In contrast to limit orders, buy stops are entered above the current market price; sell stops are entered below it.

STRADDLE

An option strategy involving a simultaneous long or short positions of both put and call option contracts, on the same underlying security and same series designation.

STRANGLE

An option strategy that involves writing a call and a put with different strike prices on the same underlying security.

STREET NAME

A term describing securities that are registered in the name of a brokerage firm, bank, or depository.

STRIKE PRICE

Also known as exercise price, it is the stated price per share at which the underlying asset may be purchased or sold by the option holder upon exercising of the options contract.

SUBJECT QUOTE

A quote given to show the current market status, not to be taken as a firm's ask or bid.

SUBORDINATED DEBENTURE

A type of debenture whose claim to interests and principal comes after those of regular debentures and other debt securities.

SUBSCRIPTION RIGHT

A stockholder's right to maintain his percentage of ownership in the company, given the opportunity to buy newly issued stock before the general public.

SUBSEQUENT INVESTMENT

The minimum amount that may be invested in a mutual fund following an initial investment.

SUPPORT (SUPPORT LEVEL)

A term used in technical analysis, describing a price level at which a security has had difficulty falling below.

SYMBOL

An abbreviation designated for publicly traded companies to facilitate identifying the security in exchanges.

❐

T

TAKEOVER

The acquisition of control over a corporation by another company, either through hostile or friendly means.

TARGET FUND

A mutual fund containing bonds that all mature in a single year, giving the entire fund a terminal maturity in that year.

TAX ANTICIPATION NOTE

A municipal note issued in anticipation of revenues from a future tax.

TAX-EXEMPT BONDS

Government securities whose interest is exempted from income tax.

TECHNICAL ANALYSIS

A method of evaluating securities by relying on market data, such as price charts and volume to predict future market trends. It is believed that investor psychology has a significant influence on the market, creating patterns that can be used to estimate whether the price of a security will rise or fall. In contrast to fundamental analysis, understanding of a company's intrinsic value is not necessary for technical analysis.

TENDER OFFER

The offer made by one company or individual for shares of another company, in the form of cash or stock.

TENURE

Duration since the current manager took over the fund.

TERM MATURITY

Bonds of an issue that mature on the same date.

TERM STRUCTURE OF INTEREST RATES

A graph representing the yield to maturity of treasury securities at identified years of maturity.

TICKER

A digital scrolling display showing prices and volume of traded securities.

TICK INDICATOR

An indicator of market trend, based on the number of stocks whose last trade was on an uptick or a downtick.

TIME HORIZON (INVESTMENT HORIZON)

The expected length of time an investor will allow to meet financial goals.

TIME VALUE

The portion of an option's premium that is attributed by the amount of time remaining until the expiration date of the option contract.

TOTAL ASSETS

Total sum of current assets plus total long-term assets.

TOTAL DEBT-TO-EQUITY RATIO

A capitalisation ratio calculated as current liabilities plus long-term debt divided by shareholders' equity.

TOTAL LIABILITIES

Accounting term referring to total current liabilities plus long-term debt and deferred taxes.

TOTAL RETURN

The price change (capital gains) plus dividend return for a stock over the last year.

TOTAL RETURN (MUTUAL FUNDS)

The combined return of a fund, including distributed and undistributed income and capital gains after taking into account all fees and expenses.

TOTAL REVENUE

Total sales and other revenues for a specific period.

TRADE

A transaction involving one party buying a security from another party.

TRADE CONFIRMATION

A verification with information concerning a transaction, sent to the client on or before the first business day following the trade date.

TRADE DATE

The date on which a trade occurs. In most stock exchanges, settlement date is 3 business days after the trade date.

TRADING RANGE

The difference between the high and low prices at which a security was traded during a period of time.

TRAILING P/E RATIO

The ratio of a stock's latest closing price divided by last reported annual earnings per share.

TRANSFER

The process by which securities are re-registered to new owners.

TRANSFER AGENT

An agent employed by a corporation or mutual fund to maintain a record of share ownership and transactions.

TREASURY DIRECT

The program which allows investors to purchase new issues of treasury bills, notes, and bonds directly from the Federal Reserve.

TREASURY NOTES (T-NOTES)

Government-issued debt security that pays interests semi-annually, maturing in two to ten years.

TRUST INDENTURE

A written agreement between a corporation and its debt-holders stating interest rates, maturity dates, collateral, etc.

TURNOVER RATIO

A measure of how frequently a fund's portfolio is traded or expressed as a percentage. For example, a fund with a 50% turnover generally changes the composition of approximately half the portfolio each year.

TYPE

The classification of an option contract as either a put or a call.

❐

U

UNCOVERED CALL

A short call option position in which the writer of the call does not own shares of underlying security of the option contract.

UNCOVERED PUT

A short put option position in which the writer of the put does not have a short position or the underlying security of the option contract.

UNDERLYING

The security on which options are being bought or sold.

UNDERWRITER (INVESTMENT BANKER)

An intermediary between the offering institution and the investing public, bringing the new issues to the market while charging the issuer a fee for the services provided.

UNDERWRITING

The process by which investment bankers bring new issues to the market.

UNDERWRITING MANAGER

The lead firm in a group of underwriters responsible for a new issue.

UNIT

A package of securities, such as a bond and warrant that become separable at a later date.

UNLISTED SECURITY

A security that has not met the requirements to be listed on an exchange.

UNWIND

An advanced option order used to intentionally close an existing buy/write or sell/write position.

UPTICK

A listed equity trade at a price that is higher than that of the last transaction.

❐

V

VOLATILITY

A relative measure of a security's price movement during a specific time period, calculated mathematically using standard deviation of daily price changes.

VOLUME

The total number of shares of a stock traded during a specific time period. High volumes usually correspond to new announcements regarding the company.

VOTING TRUST

The deposit of shares, along with transfer of voting rights to a trustee for a specific period of time.

❐

W

WARRANT

A security which entitles the purchase of a specific amount of common stock at a specific price. Most warrants expire after a certain date, but some never expire.

WEIGHTED-AVERAGE MATURITY

The arithmetic mean of maturities of securities held by a mutual fund.

WHITE KNIGHT

A company that rescues another in financial trouble, preventing a takeover by a hostile bid.

WITHDRAWAL PLAN

A plan to automatically redeem mutual fund holdings and have proceeds mailed directly to the investor.

WORKOUT QUOTE

A price at which the trader believes a security can be bought or sold if given time to find a market.

WORST 3-MONTH RETURN

The fund's worst three-month return measured in rolling periods over the past five years.

WRITER

The seller of an option contract.

W-TYPE BOTTOM

Two consecutive bottom shapes on a price or indicator chart, resembling the alphabet W.

❐

Y

YELLOW SHEETS

Wholesale quote sheets for corporate bonds used by dealers.

YIELD (BOND)

The interests earned on a bond investment. If the security was bought on the primary market, the yield will be equal to the interest rate. If the bond was acquired on the secondary market, the yield could be higher or lower depending whether the bond was bought at a premium or discount to face value.

YIELD (STOCK)

The annual rate of return on a stock as paid in dividends, calculated by dividing the latest dividend rate by the latest closing price, expressed as a percentage.

YIELD CURVE

This is a graph showing the yields for different bond maturities.

YIELD ELBOW

The point on the yield curve that indicates the year at which the economy's highest interest rates occur.

YIELD TO CALL

The percentage rate of a callable bond or note if one were to buy and hold the security until the next available call date.

YIELD TO MATURITY

The yield received by the holder of a debt security at maturity, taking into account any gain or loss of principal.

❐

Z

ZERO-COUPON BONDS

Bonds that do not pay interest periodically. Instead, these bonds are purchased at a discount and held to maturity, when all compounded interest is paid and the bondholder collects the face value of the bond.

ZERO-COUPON CD

A certificate of deposit that pays interest only upon maturity.

ZERO-MINUS TICK

A stock trade at a price that is equal to the preceding trade but lower than the last different price.

ZERO-PLUS TICK

A stock trade at a price that is equal to the preceding trade but higher than the last different price.

❐

Acronyms & Abbreviations

GENERAL FINANCIAL ABBREVIATIONS AND ACRONYMS

AIR	–	Assumed Interest Rate
APR	–	Annual Percentage Rate
ARM	–	Adjustable Rate Mortgage
CD	–	Certificate of Deposit
EFT	–	Electronic Funds Transfer
ETF	–	Exchange-Traded Funds
FDIC	–	Federal Deposit Insurance Corporation
FOREX	–	Foreign Exchange
FRB	–	Federal Reserve Board
GNP	–	Gross National Product
IRA	–	Individual Retirement Account
LOI	–	Letter Of Intent
MMKT	–	Money Market
NAV	–	Net Asset Value
PSP	–	Profit-Sharing Plan
REIT	–	Real Estate Investment Trust
SEC	–	Securities Exchange Commission
TSA	–	Tax-Sheltered Annuity
YTM	–	Yield To Maturity

BANKING AND FINANCE

CAGR – Compound Annual Growth Rate
CAPEX – Capital Expenditures
COB – Close Of Business
EPS – Earnings Per Share
LLC – Limited Liability Company
MTD – Month-to-Date
NAV – Net Asset Value
NCND – Non-Circumvent and Non-Disclosure
NDA – Non-Disclosure Agreement
P&L – Profit and Loss
P/E – Price-to-Earnings Ratio
QTD – Quarter-to-Date
ROA – Return On Assets
ROCE – Return On Capital Employed
ROE – Return On Equity
ROI – Return On Investment
ROIC – Return On Invested Capital
RONA – Return On Net Assets
ROS – Return On Sales
SIV – Structured Investment Vehicle
TSR – Total Shareholder Return
WC – Working Capital
YTD – Year-To-Date

DESIGNATIONS' ABBREVIATIONS IN BUSINESS AND FINANCE

CAO – Chief Accounting Officer
CFA – Chartered Financial Analyst
CFM – Certified Financial Manager
CFO – Chief Financial Officer

CIA – Certified Internal Auditor
CISA – Certified Information Systems Auditor
CMA – Certified Management Accountant
CMO – Chief Marketing Officer
COO – Chief Operating Officer
CPA – Certified Public Accountant
CPP – Certified Payroll Professional
CSO – Chief Security Officer
CTO – Chief Technology Officer

STOCK MARKET ABBREVIATIONS

ADX – Abu Dhabi Securities Exchange
ADR – Annual Dividend Ratio
ADTV – Average Daily Trading Volume
AEX – Amsterdam Stock Exchange
AMEX – American Stock Exchange
APT – Arbitrage Pricing Theory
ASX – Australian Securities Exchange
BBV – Bolivian Stock Exchange
BEAM – Bonds, Equity, and Money
BGSE – Bangalore Stock Exchange
BSE – Bombay Stock Exchange
CAPM – Capital Asset Pricing Model
CB – Current Bid
CGT – Capital Gains Tax
CMP – Current Market Price
DJIA – Dow Jones Industrial Average
DP – Depository Participant
DPS – Dividends Per Share
DY – Dividend Yield
EMH – Efficient Market Hypothesis
EPS – Earnings Per Share
F & O – Futures and Options

FACTS – Fully Automated Computer Trading System
FDI – Foreign Direct Investment
FII – Foreign Institutional Investor
FOF – Fund of Funds
SEHK – Stock Exchange of Hong Kong Limited
IPO – Initial Public Offering
IR – Investor Relations
IRA – Individual Retirement Account
IRR – Internal Rate of Return
JSE – Johannesburg Stock Exchange
KASE – Kazakhstan Stock Exchange
KSE – Kyrgyz Stock Exchange
LSE – London Stock Exchange
MCAP – Market Cap (Capitalisation)
MF – Mutual Fund
NASDAQ – National Association of Securities Dealers Automated Quotation
NSE – Nairobi Stock Exchange
NSE – Nigerian Stock Exchange
NSE – National Stock Exchange
NYSE – New York Stock Exchange
NZX – New Zealand Exchange
ODIN – Open Dealer Integrated (Trading) Network
OTCEI – Over the Counter Exchange of India
PFD – Preferred Stock
PPF – Public Provident Fund
QTE – Quote
ROA – Return On Assets
ROI – Return On Investment
ROMI – Return On Market Investment
ROP – Return Of Premium
RSP – Retirement Savings Plan
SENSEX – Bombay Stock Exchange Sensitive Index

SIP	–	Systematic Investment Plan
SSE	–	Shanghai Stock Exchange
SZSE	–	Shenzhen Stock Exchange
T + 1	–	Trade Date Plus One Day
T + 3	–	Trade Date Plus Three Days
TWSE	–	Taiwan Stock Exchange
VAR	–	Value at Risk
WMA	–	Weekly Moving Average
XD	–	Ex-dividend
XRT	–	Ex-rights

❑❑❑